WAR THROUGH THE PINES

From The Earth Series
Book 2

D.W. PATTERSON

Twenty-third Printing – July 2026
ISBN: 9798223502487

Future Chron Publishing

Hard Science Fiction – Old School.

To Sarah

ACKNOWLEDGMENTS

Ideas about the geopolitics of the war described herein follow closely those outlined in the book *The Next 100 Years* by George Friedman, highly recommended.

WAR THROUGH THE PINES

CHAPTER 1

Donner Jackson was thirteen years old when his family moved to the remote valley. At first, he found it lonely and frightening, the way the wind howled through the pines at night sounding like an animal alive. And the darkness, Donner found it all-enveloping, almost suffocating. It was too dark, almost too dark to sleep.

Donner busied himself with getting a satellite internet connection so that his nights wouldn't seem quite so lonely. Although Donner's dad, Jack, was too busy to help, Donner had no trouble setting up the old mini-dish and modem bought at a yard sale. The dishes and their electronics were cheap now since the introduction of the omni-directional antennas a few years earlier. The new antennas didn't require the careful alignment that the dishes needed. But cheap was good on Donner's budget.

He used his dad's metalworking equipment in the barn to attach the dish to his telescope mount for accurate tracking. It wasn't necessary to track the satellites in the array, but it would bring in a stronger, steadier signal and consequently, a higher data rate. If he could get the data rate high enough, he could even play online games again with his old friends.

Luckily, the house was located across the grassy field from the mountains and slightly above the valley floor which kept the peaks from masking the satellites Donner needed. He worked at locking his makeshift antenna onto their signals. He managed to catch an occasional signal. And the more he worked on his system the better it got at tracking and locking onto the satellites.

The next step was decoding the signal. Donner would use his personal AI device, called an ANI (Artificial Narrow Intelligence) or Annie. Annies could learn to do anything with a little software and a lot of machine learning. They learned by training on data sets that the user submitted to them. It was very important to use complete, correct, and valid data. Good data, good result; bad data, bad result. Donner's Annie was a portable device but still had the power to decode the data streams if enough samples from the satellites could be acquired to train it.

Because of the obstacles the mountains offered, Donner had a twenty-minute window with each satellite which was reduced somewhat as the dish took time to lock onto the signal. So it was hit or miss for a while. But slowly Donner built a database of satellite data. And his Annie became better and better at decoding the data.

Once his Annie could decode the data sufficiently Donner was quick to renew his gameplay. His friends were happy to have him back online because he was a good game player, although they would kid him about being out in the sticks. Donner also got his shows and movies and access to online bookstores again. Unlike his friends, Donner had a love for physical books. His mother, Phylicia, found Donner's latest purchase one morning when a delivery drone landed in the front yard with a package addressed to her son. She was upset that Donner would be so extravagant when he could easily have downloaded the e-book version.

When she told his dad about their son's exploits, his dad suggested to Donner that it might be a good idea to get the family's media Annie online so that his mom could catch some of her shows too, Donner could charge the service to his father's credit account. Donner did so and the incident faded from family memory.

With his dad's support, Donner soon had two dishes running. One could be receiving from the satellite currently visible while the other was locking onto the following satellite in the array. Because of the high data rate he was getting, he was even able to meet up with his old friends using his virtual reality helmet, almost feeling as if he was back home. It helped relieve the loneliness.

The setup worked great unless his mother was recording something off one of the satellites, then he was back to one dish. He solved this by talking his dad into buying a cheap used dish, amplifier and tracking mount and adding it to his setup. Now he had at least two dishes at all times to monitor his internet satellites.

Then he got the idea that he could use his setup to receive more television channels for his mom if he could receive the satellites in geosynchronous orbit, about ten times further away. All he had to do was combine the signals from his dishes to get enough signal strength to pull in the weaker signals. In effect, he would create one large dish out of his three smaller ones.

He talked to his dad.

"Son," replied his father. "You are right in theory but in practice that is a very difficult engineering job. And professional equipment that could do something like that costs in the five-figure range. It would be easier and probably cheaper to get one of the newer omni-directional antennas and the appropriate electronics."

But not as much fun, thought Donner. "But if I wanted to try, what would I need?"

"Well," said his dad. "You would need to phase lock the signals from the different antennas so that they don't destructively interfere. You want the signals to synchronize so that they build in amplitude like ocean waves approaching the shore. To do that you will need a super-accurate clock that would allow you to compensate for position and tracking errors between the dishes. So, it's quite a challenge, isn't it?"

"Yeah," said Donner. "I'm going to have to think about it for a while."

CHAPTER 2

To Staff Sergeant Emily Rosen they weren't just sleek flying machines. The hypersonics were her babies. She programmed the onboard flight ANI and nurtured the "beast," the hypersonic scramjet that put the hyper in hypersonic.

And every one of the more than thirty hypersonics located at the secret west Pacific island airbase had a personality as far as Emily was concerned. She was sure that "Supersonic," as she had christened one of her charges, would no doubt make a success of any mission he was assigned. But as for "Lex" well, he would do okay as long as the others led the way. Lex hadn't exactly shown himself a leader.

Most of the squad were kinetic energy weapons. The size of a small fighter jet, they would deliver their bulk against the target at hypersonic speeds. The resultant destructive force would pierce any target no matter how hardened it had been constructed. A couple of hypersonics in the squadron provided reconnaissance, they would help guide the others if local conditions required. They were the only two that might return from the mission. Emily had named them "Looker" and "Booker".

She was talking to Looker now.

"Looker report status," Emily said to her Annie which relayed the request to Looker.

"Status nominal. Download of latest reconnaissance mapping from DOD satellite is complete. Integration into existing database is proceeding. Estimated completion, sixteen hundred hours."

"Looker, memory upgrade sufficient for new information download?"

"Yes, a ten percent buffer will be maintained."

Emily worried over that number a moment.

"Looker, how much did this last download decrease memory capacity?"

"Memory capacity decreased by five percent."

Damn, thought Emily. Even with all my efforts, memory is still going to be a problem. I can't believe the red tape involved in procuring upgrades. I ask for a thousand terabytes and I get ten.

Okay relax, she said to herself. Time to go off-script.

When Emily went off-script she meant she was going to solve the problem through her own efforts. The brass didn't need to know.

"You still talking to machines Sgt. Rosen?" asked a voice behind her.

Emily turned to see Lieutenant Warner.

"Sir," said Emily as she saluted. "I find the audio interface far more efficient than a keyboard."

"Yes, you've made that clear to me and the other officers Sgt. Rosen. But it still seems strange to me."

"Sir, I can assure you that there is nothing strange about it. These machines have the same intelligence as the Annies most of us carry. And sometimes more," said Emily, referring to her unauthorized modifications to the ANI in the aircraft which only she knew about.

"Well, carry on," said the Lieutenant.

"Yes sir," said Emily saluting.

After the Lieutenant had left the hangar, Emily said quietly, "Good thing he has a great head of hair, makes him at least look like an officer."

"I agree," said Looker.

Emily laughed.

CHAPTER 3

While Donner researched the electronics needed to get his antennas to sync, he helped his father around the farm. Each week brought a delivery of some new equipment to make the farm more self-sufficient. They soon had the robotic vegetable gardeners working. Then they automated the water purification and distribution system, including the well, stream and the rainwater cisterns. The fruit orchard was planted and attended to by a specialized robot. The work for Donner and his dad soon devolved into keeping the machines in good condition and updating their programming.

Working on his antennas and helping his dad didn't keep Donner completely occupied. He also explored around the farm and the adjacent woods and soon became comfortable with his new surroundings. He missed his friends but realized how much of their time together had been spent playing games online which they could still do.

These exploratory wanderings were something that he came to look forward to. The woods were always changing according to the weather or time of day, the nearby stream was quiet or raucous according to the last rain, and the birds and deer he saw were mostly unwary of him as if he were not the intruder, he thought himself to be. He made it a goal to learn more about the plants and animals in this part of the country.

Just after Donner turned fourteen it was time for school to start. He took his classes at home online with his mother as his tutor. Donner's mother was well qualified to teach with one degree in Biology and another in Mathematics. She had even completed much of a Ph.D. in Microbiology before a disagreement with her adviser forced her out of the program. In fact, she and her husband had worked in the same lab, becoming close when Jack also was forced out of the program because of illness.

It was just before the end of the school year that Donner first got his project online. The electronics he designed with the help of his Annie used predictive look-ahead to estimate the necessary phase adjustment for each antenna signal. This look-ahead design gave the tracking motors the time they needed to maintain a lock on the satellite signal. This reduced the corrections necessary to something that a fast processor, such as the one in his Annie, could digitize and then use to eliminate the remaining errors mathematically.

Donner set the system up for nightly surveys of the geosynchronous region with an analysis the next day using his Annie. It wasn't long until he found a very unusual signal.

CHAPTER 4

Lieutenant Brently Armstrong had always wanted to go into outer space. But he hadn't expected it to be his first assignment after graduating from the Space Force Academy. No doubt his double major in Astronautics and Physics, not to mention his summer internships at the NASA Ames Research Center, contributed to his selection.

The ride up had been a thrill. Chemical rockets might be old-fashioned compared with the Maglev system, which rail-gunned cargo into orbit, but wow, they were still a kick to ride. Arriving in geosynchronous orbit the spacecraft docked with the Space Defense Platform and Brently transferred down the short docking tube to be welcomed aboard.

After a quick orientation lecture, he was shown his quarters. The transition from the zero gravity of the docking section to the one-third gravity of the living quarters seemed natural to Brently as he traversed the ladder. Once he was in the wheel-shaped rotating section which was sandwiched between the equipment and station keeping booms, he simply turned his body one-hundred and eighty degrees and continued 'down' the ladder. The rotating section provided enough gravity for people to do most of their daily activities normally. Besides personnel quarters, also in this section was the exercise area, workrooms and the mess hall.

Brently was impressed with the number of robotic servers aboard. Most were about the size of a roll-about storage bin, some with drawers, some with doors. They would exit from a room and cross to the opposite wall and follow it to their destination. Brently later learned that they navigated by the colored strips and numbers painted on the floors and walls as well as a wireless hookup. They carried tools, food, clothes, anything that a station resident would need. They were all business, not stopping unless someone or something got in their way.

Stowing his personal effects, he headed off to workroom seven to meet his immediate boss.

Brently buzzed the door and heard someone call, enter. Pressing the button again rotated the latch and opened the door to reveal his working quarters. The workroom was large enough to notice the station curvature. Seeing someone at the far end Brently snapped to attention and said, “Lieutenant Brently Armstrong reporting for duty, sir.”

“At ease Armstrong,” came the reply. “In this workroom we are all equal. Outside this room you can salute me if you want.”

“Yes sir,” said Brently reflexively.

“My name is Eric Fermion, and yes I know that a fermion is a particle so you can leave the jokes outside if you don't mind.”

“Of course, sir.”

“In here call me Eric please, we haven't enough personnel in our department to maintain the usual protocol.”

“Of course, Eric.”

“Now let me explain to you what needs to be done before we go live. Most of the installation work is finished. But we still need to calibrate our instruments. I'm going to ask you to work with the electromagnetics, which is the EM sensors. The electromagnetic fields up here are small but significant. They could provide us with advanced warning of a change in the space weather or even an attack. So, we want the EM sensors calibrated to a fine degree and dependable.

“And let me introduce you to our robotic assistants. This is Test and this is Measurement, as I have named them. They may assist you in whatever way you need.”

The robots were similar except one was trimmed in red and the other in blue. Modeled on human anatomy they had stereoscopic vision, two powerful arms with end attachments that could be replaced as needed, according to the job. They also had two wheels, like the old self-balancing scooters, upon which they moved. They stood about five feet but could extend their height to seven feet if needed.

“Pleased to meet you Brently,” said Test. “Please call me Tess.”

"Just call me Mess," added Measurement.

"Good to meet you and call me Brently please."

Dr. Fermion added, "They came up with the nicknames themselves."

He continued, "Brently I picked you because of your experiences at Ames, I think you are uniquely qualified for this job."

"Thank you Eric. I'll get right on it."

"Slow down a minute. It's my dinner time. Would you like to join me in the mess hall."

"Sure Eric."

After dinner, Dr. Fermion excused himself to his quarters. Brently decided to get an early start in his duties and returned to the workroom.

The real trick with calibrating EM sensors isn't so much picking up the electromagnetic fields you want, but not picking up the fields you don't want. It was difficult not to pick up EM fields with so much electrical and electronic equipment around. So, the known fields had to be canceled in order that unknown EM fields could be detected.

Brently worked well into the night calibrating the sensors. He had identified and nulled out almost all the station's EM sources except for a very small remainder.

Tess had been working with him. "I think that's all we can do tonight, Tess. I'm getting too tired to continue."

"Very well Brently, why don't you go ahead to your quarters, and I will finish up before powering down."

"Okay Tess, see you in the morning."

The next morning Dr. Fermion was in the workroom before Brently. He was observing the EM sensors and talking to Tess when Brently came into the room.

"Good morning Brently," said Eric.

"Good morning," said Tess.

"Good morning, Eric, Tess. I see you are inspecting my EM sensors."

"Yes," said Eric. "Tess told me you two worked pretty late to get them calibrated this far. I see a slight residual in the readings; you have a bit more to do?"

"Yeah, I tried to get them completely zeroed but that stubborn signal remains."

"Well, you seem to have made an excellent start. If we can get these sensors online today the General will be very pleased."

"I'm gonna try," said Brently.

Brently continued his calibrations which went quicker this time as Tess was able to handle some of the work. By comparing readings in different sections of the station with external sensor readings and noting the correlations, he was again able to reduce the remaining sensor reading to almost zero but not quite. Then, just as he was about to let out a string of invectives not befitting a military officer, the reading dropped to zero.

Brently stared at the readout. There was no way that it could be a coincidence he thought.

"Tess, that can't be a coincidence."

"I agree, highly improbable."

Measurement came over, "I have finished my assignment, I am free to help here if needed."

"Thanks Mess," said Brently. "Well let's get busy."

They set about to again recalibrate all the sources, something that took them well into the afternoon. When finished the reading was as before, zero. Brently told Dr. Fermion about his experience.

"It just went away?" asked Eric.

"Yes. And I haven't seen it since. Maybe some machinery cycling on and off?"

"Possibly. Brently, I want you to make a correlation between readings and the machinery causing those readings, then I want you to start logging the sensor outputs. Make it one-second intervals. Let's get a history of this signal. Maybe then we can correlate it to something onboard the station."

"And if not?"

"Well, then we take it to the General."

CHAPTER 5

The antennas had locked in a southwesterly direction and stopped moving. Donner figured that the signal came from a region of geosynchronous orbit that was above and slightly off the coast of equatorial South America. He made an estimate of the satellite's orbital elements and consulted a database of orbiting satellites but found no match.

Donner soon came to realize that the signal was not aimed at him but was spillover from a signal that was probably aimed directly below the satellite. The signal strength was such that Donner's antennas had to be almost exactly on target to attain lock. Donner thought he must be in a zone where the signal reinforced, but that zone couldn't be too wide or surely someone else would have already identified this anomaly. The signal also seemed to use a spread spectrum technique, but his Annie easily accounted for that.

Anyway, receiving the signal was one thing, making sense of it was something else. He was sure it was encrypted and cracking the encryption would be challenging. Donner set his Annie up decrypting the signal but made no progress. He didn't know at the time that it would take several weeks.

After school was out for the year, Donner became serious about decrypting the strange signal. He had quite a large amount of data stored which had been collecting for several weeks. He decided that the best approach to decryption would be to farm out portions to his friends and let them set their ANI devices to work. He would edit the snippets, keeping them short, to keep from giving away too much information if someone did decrypt it.

Donner prepared several different samples. His Annie sent the samples to his friend's Annies. They immediately put their Annies to the task of decoding the samples. Decryption algorithms on their devices would run in the background during the day and evening, taking over all the CPU cycles when the owners didn't need them.

Donner then setup the Annies to run as a wide area network over the internet. He wrote supervisory software that allowed them to exchange algorithms, trade samples and build a common, shared database of results. It took hundreds of CPU hours before the first sample was decrypted and exchanged among all the devices. Further results came quickly as the Annies developed a voting system to choose the most probable decrypt. But the decrypted signal only led to another mystery.

The samples were in a language that Donner nor any of his friends or their Annies recognized. Donner found an online translation website and scanned in the language samples. He then set the website to translate the samples into English. The translation database identified the samples as a dialect of Japanese but gave no other information and served up a very incomplete translation.

After much research and false leads, Donner found the solution to the unusual Japanese. It turned out to be a dialect spoken on Hachijojima and Aogashima, islands south of Tokyo. It was the Hachijo dialect, and it was quite divergent from primary Japanese, retaining many features inherited from ancient Eastern Japanese.

Donner, with the help of his Annie, labored several days to complete a manual translation of the snippets. The importance of his discovery slowly dawned on him, he realized he would have to show his dad.

CHAPTER 6

Donner's dad read the translated messages with increasing concern. When he finished reading, he looked at Donner and shook his head.

"Well Donner, first I have to say that your work on this project is top-notch. What you have done here reminds me of my experiences in viral research years ago. But of course, you also did the hardware design. This is college-level if not graduate-level work."

Donner was silent but smiling.

"Anyway, you certainly have something here. If I read this correctly, I think it has to do with a manned space platform. And I think it is not an authorized transmission."

"What do you think it means dad?"

"I think it is a message from an embedded informant."

"You mean a spy?"

"Yes, son. I think we have a spy. See here," he said, pointing to one of the decrypted snippets.

"This looks like a technical description of something, which I think is a weapons system. I doubt that the owners of this platform would be transmitting such technical details. I believe you've discovered a top-secret space platform Donner. Apparently undetectable if not for this unauthorized transmission."

"Do you think it has something to do with Japan dad? I mean it is a dialect of Japanese."

"Yes, and it is an obscure dialect which would be difficult to interpret for most people, even other Japanese. But I don't think we can say who is behind it. The chosen language could just be a way to throw off someone who happened to decode the message. I think we are going to have to get some outside help Donner, before we take our next step. I have a friend in Space Command I went to engineering school with, I think I'll give him a call. He might be able to offer us some advice on how to proceed."

Colonel Reginald Allen listened to Donner's father explain what his son had found.

After listening to Jack Jackson, Colonel Allen said, "I'll say one thing Jack, that is quite an enterprising young man you have there, Space Command would be proud to have him someday."

"Thank you Reg," said Jack. "He certainly keeps himself busy with these little projects of his. So what do you think we should do now?"

"Could you and your son fly out to Colorado Springs and present your findings to a few people I believe may be able to help us?"

"I think we could arrange that; Donner is out of school for a few more weeks. When do you want to set this up?"

"Let me check everyone's schedule Jack and I'll get back to you, okay?"

"Sure Reg, just let us know, goodbye," said Jack.

When his dad told him Donner said, "That's great dad, can we fly ourselves out or do we have to take a commercial airline?"

"You love to fly, don't you son?"

"Sure, what do you think?"

"Okay we'll see what Colonel Allen comes up with and if we can get your mother's approval, we'll fly ourselves out there."

"Thanks dad," said Donner with a big grin.

CHAPTER 7

Emily was curious. Something was going on. The top brass on the island seemed to be scrambling. She had been told to make sure her fleet was ready at a moment's notice. There was nothing on the nets that seemed out of the ordinary. She would just have to wait until they believed she had a need to know.

In the meantime, she was arranging for the squadron to fly an evaluation mission. The objective would be to scout and find a target ship five hundred miles out from the base. The mission would depend heavily on Looker and Booker for real-time on-site target and threat determination. The other hypersonics would be evaluated on their flight performance over target as directed by the reconnaissance hypersonics.

Emily and her team had worked overtime since the readiness command to get the hypersonics in shape. Maintenance was always a concern, but this mission had a profile that would stress the hypersonics far beyond any previous evaluation. Emily was particularly concerned with losing any telemetry data. She absolutely wanted to be aware of the hypersonics' flight status at all times. She drove her team to finish all the preventive maintenance possible that might ensure nothing would go wrong.

The day of the evaluation Emily was up at zero three hundred having only slept fitfully for some four hours. According to schedule, the flight would take off a half-hour after dawn. Looker and Booker would quickly accelerate to Mach 7, or over five-thousand miles-per-hour, arriving at the target site some six minutes later. The rest of the flight would boost to Mach 4, over three-thousand miles-per-hour, arriving at the target a few minutes after Looker and Booker. This would give the strike hypersonics the needed margin to adjust course if the reconnaissance hypersonics deemed it necessary.

Exactly at a half-hour after dawn, the flight began to take off. Because of their highly networked and autonomous operation, the entire flight of some thirty hypersonics was in the air in just over a minute. After watching the takeoff Emily headed for her monitoring post.

Thirty streams of telemetry were coming into Emily and the other monitors. Emily herself was monitoring Looker, Booker and Supersonic. The data showed smooth acceleration as the jet engines took the flight up to almost Mach 4. Then the scramjets took over. For most of the hypersonics, their velocity settled at just over Mach 4. But for Looker and Booker, the velocity climbed almost exponentially to Mach 7 before settling. The scramjets were working flawlessly.

Because of the speed, it wasn't long until Looker and Booker were within sight of the target, an old navy ship that had been towed to the site and set adrift. Immediately telemetry from Looker increased.

Emily's Annie began to speak. “Looker to Sg, Looker to Sg”.

Surprised, Emily could only answer as she had many times before, “Sg here.”

“Sg we have found the target. Threat level is low. We are broadcasting location and speed data of target to flight. They should be making needed course corrections now.”

Emily saw this in Supersonics' telemetry as he corrected his preflight track. But Emily was more worried about the extra telemetry that Looker was sending, the audio link.

“Looker this is Sg,” she said into her Annie. “Please advise need for extra telemetry.”

“Looker to Sg, determination was made that this was most efficient comm link.”

Emily now remembered her conversation with Lieutenant Warner when he caught her talking to Looker. She had insisted that a direct audio link was most efficient. Looker had been listening and reached that conclusion also.

But that was not under combat conditions, thought Emily.

"Understand Looker. But telemetry data may be compromised by added burden of . . ."

Just then the door to the monitoring room burst open. Lieutenant Warner was in the lead and behind him was the General and the rest of the brass.

"Sergeant Rosen!" Warner yelled. "What is the meaning of this additional telemetry from the reconnaissance craft?"

Before Emily could answer Looker said, "Sg this is Looker, flight has made its pass at the target. I estimate that there is one-hundred percent annihilation of target. Over."

Emily turned from Warner and said to her Annie, "Looker this is Sg, that is affirmative, well done. Make course for home and return to base."

"Understood."

Emily turned to Warner.

"Well?" he said.

"Sir, it was the determination of flight ops that this would enhance the mission. As the Lieutenant has just heard mission goals have been achieved thus far."

"That is not the answer I was hoping for. Who was responsible for this 'enhancement'?"

Emily thought; she realized that an ANI making such a judgment could cost the whole squadron its readiness designation. It would be immediately taken offline until the brass understood how it could happen.

"I made the decision. But only because I thought it would be more efficient than the current procedure."

The General spoke up, "Sergeant Rosen, you are not an engineer, are you?"

"No sir."

"You did not develop the software or hardware that, by the way, the military has spent billions of dollars on, did you?"

"No sir."

"It's my understanding that your job is to keep the squadron in flight condition. Any changes or improvements to procedures should be made by authorized personnel only, don't you agree?"

Emily knew what was coming. "Yes sir."

"Sergeant Rosen for your unauthorized change in procedures you are now on report. An inquiry will be made into this matter. You are relieved of duty."

"Yes sir." Emily saluted smartly and left the monitoring room.

CHAPTER 8

Colonel Allen came through with a meeting date and Donner, and his dad were on their way to the nearest airport a couple of counties over. Jack had already had his plane readied for the trip. Six hundred miles to Joplin, Missouri; refuel, and another six hundred miles to Colorado Springs Airport. The trip should take about eight hours in flight.

Donner was still too young for his student flight certificate, but he knew his dad would let him do some of the flying. The flight was without incident with Donner flying while his dad navigated. Jack was old enough that he could still use the VOR stations (a type of radio ranging system used for aircraft navigation) that remained in operation to check their course. Donner thought that was pretty antiquated since their plane and each of their Annies had a GPS. Jack brought them into Colorado Springs with plenty of daylight left. They checked in to a motel and after a pizza for dinner, they turned in to get an early start the following morning.

The meeting with Colonel Allen and the others was scheduled for zero eight hundred. Jack and Donner were up by seven and had breakfast at a restaurant off Space Center Drive. They arrived at North American Aerospace Defense several minutes before their scheduled meeting.

They were shown to Colonel Allen's office where they waited. Reg Allen soon arrived and led them to a nearby conference room. There they were introduced to the other participants of the meeting.

Colonel Allen began, “Jack and Donner, I would like you to meet my operations officer, Captain Deek Lang, our intelligence liaison, Captain Joyce Sargent, and my IT officer, Lieutenant Jim Mason. This will just be a low-key inquiry. If we all agree that the information Donner has discovered warrants it, I plan to take it up with my boss Major General Longsteen. But for right now this is just an informal fact-finding discussion.

“I've explained to everyone some of what Donner has

discovered. But I wonder Donner if you would like to give some background into how you made the discovery, and the details of what you've learned?"

"Okay," said Donner somewhat nervously. "As far as the background to my discovery I was attempting to establish a reliable internet connection after my family moved to a rural location."

Donner then described his antenna setup and the mechanism he designed to achieve and maintain satellite lock which interested the operations officer quite a bit and he asked a few questions.

Next, he turned to the signal he found and how he had set up the wide-area network that decrypted it. The IT officer then became curious. Finally, Donner told them about how he had discovered the Japanese dialect the messages used. The intelligence officer nodded approvingly.

Donner finished his review in about ten minutes and then passed out copies of the decrypted and translated messages he had intercepted. The three officers and Colonel Allen seemed to be suitably impressed. Jack was smiling.

Colonel Allen spoke up, "Thank you Donner. I think I speak for all of us when I say that your work is quite impressive. Now, I've arranged for you and your dad to tour our facilities as well as the airbase and the Space Museum. My staff and I will discuss your findings, and I will meet with you and your father for dinner at seven tonight. Okay with you Donner?"

"Sure, Colonel Allen and thank you for arranging all this."

"Your welcome Donner."

Colonel Allen's adjutant came in to escort Donner and his dad on the tour.

After a long day of touring the facilities and the museums, Donner and his dad met Colonel Allen at the Peterson AFB Club for dinner. Colonel Allen ordered a drink for Jack and himself and a soft drink for Donner before beginning the discussion.

"Well Donner," said the Colonel. "How was the tour?"

"Excellent sir. The facilities and space museum tours were awesome. And I really liked eating lunch in the airplane restaurant, the old KC-135 fuselage."

"I'm glad to hear it Donner, it is quite an antique. Now I want to talk to you and your dad about the meetings I've had today. I have to say again that everyone was very impressed with your work. I think that some of my staff would like for you to instruct them in some of your techniques."

Donner smiled from behind his soft drink.

"Jack what I would like to do is place a mobile listening post on your property. Would that be okay?"

"Of course, Reg, if you think that is for the best."

"I think so. Donner, once we get the mobile post setup, I'm going to ask you to shut down your operation. I don't want you involved in what could be an international incident. I'm afraid we are going to keep your work top secret for now."

"I understand sir."

"Good, then let's eat," said the Colonel. "The meal is on Space Command."

CHAPTER 9

Something was definitely up, thought Jason Bigley. Suddenly all his sources in the military had clammed up. He had been on to something important, something to do with orbital space. He was preparing an in-depth report for the website he worked for. Such a coup was needed as the site was in danger of shutting down.

Jason wasn't going to let that happen. He would go with what he had even though he knew his information was incomplete. He would do a write-up of the story that he had and fill in the gaps with reasonable conjecture. He would send the finished story to his military sources. If there were no objections he would put it on the website.

Jason knew the military had embarked on a program to get all its hypersonic squadrons on high alert, that he was sure of. The order had seemingly come because of an investigation being conducted by Space Command. That was the space connection. But exactly why the military was worried about space he didn't know.

He did know that the Chinese were planning massive war games and that they had space assets as well as a base on the moon. But China was technically still an ally of the United States so why this should cause an alert was unclear. That and a few other minor points was all he had so he wrote up the story and sent it to his contacts.

He waited three days.

One of his contacts, a former Colonel in Space Command called.

"You can't put out this drivel," said Colonel Sloan.

"What do you mean," said Jason. "It's all the truth, and accurate as far as I know."

"But that is the point, you don't know enough. You are jumping to conclusions. You insinuate that the Chinese are planning something that will affect the United States' access to space. But the link is not direct, it's purely circumstantial."

"Well," said Jason. "If you would like to fill me in on what I don't know I'll change the story."

"You know I can't do that. I told you when I stopped passing information that a direct request had come down."

"You're a civilian now Colonel, you don't have to follow orders."

"That's where we part company Jason. I may be a private citizen, but when I believe that something I do can bring more harm than good to the country then that is where I draw the line."

"Okay. Basically, you are telling me that I don't have the whole truth, but you and the rest of your kind aren't willing to fill me in. So, there you have it. I also have a duty to publish the truth as I know it. Maybe once it's out there the military or others like you will correct me and we, that is citizens of the country, can know what our government is up to."

"Jason, I will tell you one last time. You print this mashup of yours and you will lose all your contacts in the military. Now and in the future. We just won't trust you anymore."

"Colonel, that is your prerogative. But I have news and I will publish it."

"Goodbye Jason."

"Goodbye Colonel."

Jason was shaking when he closed his Annie. They'll see, he thought. I've got enough to publish and they know it. We'll see who becomes the pariah.

Jason's boss had read the copy. He put down his Annie and turned to Jason.

"Jason," said Max Cleveland. "You are sure of this story. This is the truth, isn't it? The whole truth."

"Yes Max. Everything I got came from a trusted source. The linkages in the information are obvious to everyone that has read the piece. I think there is enough in there to force the military out into the open about what is going on in space. The Chinese have some kind of weapons platform up there and the US military is worried enough to put our top assets on alert."

"The Chinese haven't been particularly aggressive in their space program in recent years Jason. Besides the moon base they haven't conducted any unusual tests, no secret satellites, nothing. You are accusing them, indirectly to be sure, of militarizing space. Jason that is a big, blaring headline that will be around the world in seconds. You have to guarantee me that at least that part of the story is based on solid evidence."

"I guarantee that the Chinese are up to something. I found out that much before everyone clammed up."

"Okay, it's going online tomorrow. The biggest headline we've ever run. We will either be lauded or driven out of business."

Back at his desk, Jason felt relief. He was sure he was right. The fact that no one actually confirmed it made him even more sure. The US military had been caught flat-footed, and they were trying to correct the mistake before anyone found out. Only now they wouldn't have the chance. He smiled.

CHAPTER 10

Jack and Donner spent the day after the meeting driving to nearby Cascade to take the toll road up Pikes Peak. Jack took the wheel manually once they started up the mountain. The drive up was a leisurely tour through a thick forest for the first twenty-five minutes then, almost immediately, the trees retreated from the roadside and the view became spectacular.

The road fell away on one side or the other, sometimes with just a foot or so of rocky curb. The ground was a light green for another five or ten minutes until it turned into a dirt and rock-strewn landscape. The side of the road disappeared into empty space.

Pike's Peak is a lonely mountain with no companion mountains to disguise its sheer height of fourteen thousand feet or block the tremendous views. After almost forty-five minutes they pulled into the parking lot at the peak. Patches of snow were on the ground and there were flurries, it was summer. The temperature was in the thirties, some fifty degrees colder than at the base of the mountain. Donner was glad his dad had brought him a coat.

The snow was not continuous and sometimes the sun would break through the clouds to light the view. Donner and his dad found a spot where they could eat the lunch they had packed.

After his dad distributed the food Donner said, "Dad can I ask you something?"

"What is it son?"

"Well Colonel Allen said what I had found was important and that they would follow up on it right?"

"That's right son."

"But after all the praise he gave me he still didn't tell me what he thought it meant. Do you have any idea?"

"I think that Colonel Allen wasn't at liberty to tell us what he was thinking Donner."

"Oh, I know that. But I still wonder why it is so important, don't you?"

"Yes, I do. I will tell you what I think, but it may not turn out to be right. I think that the message you intercepted came from a geosynchronous space platform that Space Command is responsible for."

"But there isn't any evidence for that."

"I know. That's why I said I could be wrong. But I think this is a platform that became operational very recently and it may be that Space Command just wants to get it set up and working before announcing anything to the public. That would be the smart way to militarize space, a *fait accompli*."

"Militarize space!" exclaimed Donner. "I thought there were international agreements against that."

"No, nothing binding, just some understandings. That's what makes it imperative to Space Command that the platform be operational and permanent before the public is told."

"So, one day there isn't and then the next day there is a military space platform, get used to it," said Donner.

"That's the way they hoped to do it. But I think what you discovered is that it is not as secret a plan as Space Command thought."

"You mean the spy on the platform."

"That's right. Well, let's finish eating and get some photos for mom, then we start back down. The trip down may be even more interesting than the trip up."

"Okay," said Donner. "One more thing dad."

"Yes?"

"This kind of thing is why you moved us to the mountains isn't it?"

"Yes it is, Donner," said Jack. "I don't like surprises."

CHAPTER 11

Lieutenant Brently Armstrong was busy. He had never been given such a difficult assignment. He was charged with finding the anomalous signal that had shown up irregularly in his data logging of the EM sensors. And he had only been given another twenty-four hours to find it. The order had come straight from the General. Something was up.

Brently started by thinking about how he could locate the source even if it wasn't transmitting. Was there any way that data analysis could show the location, or at least the area of the platform from which the signal was being generated?

He thought about the information he already knew. He knew the different sources of the electromagnetic interference which he had nulled out. He knew their relative strength which his EM sensors picked up and he knew their exact location from scouting the station.

If he could build a map of the platform and locate each noise source and its signal strength on that map, he might be able to use the data he had on the unknown source to assign it to no more than a few areas around the platform.

"Tess," he said. "We need a map of the station, do you know of any in the database?"

"Yes Brently. I'll bring up the different versions on the terminal over here and you can choose."

Brently reviewed the different station configuration diagrams and chose one to work with. He began using his Annie to correlate EM noise sources with distance from the sensors. By tagging the platform diagram with noise source, location and signal strength he developed his map.

Now it was just a matter of making an assumption about the signal strength of the unknown source...

Brently jumped as his Annie switched to a very loud alarm mode. The unknown source was back online! The Annie had learned that Brently was interested in this signal and had arranged the alarm itself.

Brently grabbed his portable EM sensor adapter and plugged it into his Annie for more precise location mining.

“Tess, the unknown source is back online. Please tell Dr. Fermion I am going to try to find the location.”

“Very well Brently, good luck.”

The Annie became a signal tracker once the external EM sensor was plugged in, the screen which now looked like a compass always pointed towards the unknown signal.

He followed the tracker out of the workroom and noticed that the signal was somewhere below him. He would have to climb to the center of the wheel and move 'down' in the direction of the lower equipment and station keeping boom.

Once in what was effectively zero gravity, Brently pulled himself in the direction of the lower boom. At the end of the long cylinder of the wheel's center, Brently pulled himself up to a viewing port from which he could see the lower boom. The view of the earth below caused a moment of vertigo.

He began to scan the boom by eye. He knew that the box or whatever it was he was looking for would have to have a long wire trailing from it. The box might be any size, though he expected it to be small, but the length of the antenna wire was fixed according to the transmission frequency. And the frequency that Brently had measured for the unknown signal would require an antenna wire of a few meters.

Brently was repeating the scan of the long boom for the third time when he thought he saw it. But he wasn't sure because the Annie's digital magnification couldn't resolve the target. If only he had a pair of real binoculars. Brently called the workroom over the intercom and asked Tess to bring a pair of binoculars.

It wasn't long before Brently saw the robot pulling itself along the handholds as he had done.

"Here are the binoculars," said Tess as she came up to Brently.

"Thanks."

Through the binoculars, he could definitely see a small box with a trailing wire.

"Tess, can you see that small box with the trailing wire about a third of the way down the boom?"

Tess moved to the window. "Yes, I see it."

We've got him, thought Brently.

"Tess, how could someone place a box such as that on the boom?"

"A human in a spacesuit or a boom management robot could have placed it there Brently."

"And to do so they would have to open this hatch?"

"I would say that is obvious," said Tess.

"Aren't all hatch accesses and robot movements logged somewhere?"

"That is correct Brently. Even my effort to bring you the binoculars has been logged. And all hatch accesses must be approved by the central computer or the officer on duty."

"Well, whoever it was that put the unauthorized transmitter out there had to go through the boom hatch or send a robot. And whichever way he did it the station logs will show. All we have to do is search those logs and question anyone associated."

Brently smiled at Tess.

The station alarm went off. Brently heard the whine of the laser weapons powering up. He went back to the window and began to look from the earth outward. He heard the pop and felt the recoil of the chemical discharge that roared out the exhaust ports of the huge three-hundred-kilowatt energy weapons. Such weapons could vaporize a six-inch thick piece of steel in seconds.

He couldn't see the attackers the lasers were firing at but he did see the remains of the chemical reaction that powered the lasers and exhausted at tremendous speed. Then he felt a strange shutter as if the station was being shaken by a giant.

The intercom crackled to life and Brently heard the all hands abandon ship alarm. He looked at Tess.

Tess said, “Hurry Brently you may have only a few minutes to reach an escape pod.”

Brently hesitated a moment, “Thanks Tess.”

He started up the nearest ladder to the wheel's perimeter. The station began a complex but repeatable vibration. Brently increased his speed.

CHAPTER 12

Donner and his dad flew back home the day after Pike's Peak. A couple of days later the 15th Mobile Space Communications Command showed up early in the morning to establish a listening post. Captain Harrison introduced himself and spoke with Jack for several minutes about where to best set up the unit. They needed a clear view of Donner's signal source and yet needed to be far enough away from the house to minimize any interference. Jack suggested they set up in the east end of the valley which was more open than the west end. Captain Harrison agreed.

The unit was set up and operating by that evening. Only six soldiers with as many robots established the base of operations. Donner went down to see the setup. The receiving dish's five-meter diameter was quite impressive deployed atop a flatbed truck. Donner introduced himself to the robotic perimeter guard who called for Captain Harrison.

Captain Harrison greeted Donner and offered to show him around the encampment. He got a quick look at the control room for the dish even though it was technically off-limits to civilians. Captain Harrison then introduced him to his technical officer, Lieutenant Jones.

Jones said, "I am pleased to meet you Donner, you are already a legend at HQ."

"What do you mean Lieutenant?" asked Donner.

"He means," said Captain Harrison interrupting, "That what you have done with essentially consumer-grade equipment impresses every technical person that learns about it, like Lieutenant Jones here."

"Well, I found a mystery is all. And I wanted to solve it. For me it was just solving a puzzle."

"Well, if we could all solve puzzles like that Donner, we wouldn't need all this equipment and training Space Command gives us. You should be proud of what you've accomplished."

"You should also be proud because it may be invaluable to

your country son," said Captain Harrison.

Donner wasn't sure what to say so he just said, "Thank you." Then his dad showed up.

"Donner your mother is looking for you. You should go on home now."

"Okay dad. Goodbye Captain Harrison, Lieutenant Jones."

Jack Jackson began talking to the soldiers as Donner walked away. Donner overheard his dad inviting them to dinner when he looked over his shoulder at the stars rising above the mountain tops. Suddenly a flare appeared through the pines between him and the mountain, it immediately dimmed and then brightened, brighter than any star. Then it faded quickly, Donner thought it was just like an explosion. He heard shouts from the encampment. That is when he knew. He knew it was his transmission source that had flared up. Donner ran to an opening among the trees and turned to stare at the sky, he saw other dimmer flares. One, then two, then another and another.

He turned back to join his dad who was walking towards him now. "Dad, you know what that was, the bright one?" he yelled.

"I think I do Donner; the dish lost the signal from your source about the time the flare happened. I also think I know what those other flares are. Let's get back to the house and use your setup. I want to see what signals we can pick up."

"What is it dad, what do you think is happening?"

"War Donner, I think it is war."

CHAPTER 13

Jason was excited. This was the first time he had ever been invited to appear on television. The host was known for favoring sensational stories. And Jason's was such.

The story had exploded on the internet. Conspiracy theorists spread it, embellished it, argued over it. In some of the stories, Jason became a Chinese agent, in others a whistleblowing hero. In all he was famous.

Jason was being prepped in makeup. Beside him was Colonel Sloan, one of Jason's former sources of information. He would be arguing against Jason's conclusions. And Jason knew that Samuel Sloan could make a good argument.

Jason was determined not to reason with the viewers but to play to their emotions. He knew his story was not tight enough to stand up to Sloan's objections. But he also knew that he only had to present himself as the reasonable party and Sloan as the nutcase to win the debate.

As they were finishing with makeup, Jason and Sloan rose from their chairs simultaneously and couldn't avoid making eye contact.

"Well Jason," said Sloan. "I guess we are going to see how well your story holds up to inspection."

"Colonel, I assure you my story will hold up under inspection as will I."

"We'll see," said the Colonel.

Jason found the lighting on the sparse set much brighter and hotter than he expected. Maybe a result of lighting the studio for the 3D super-high-definition broadcast. The set included just the three chairs and a high desk. The host on one side, his two guests on the other. Jason was afraid he might start sweating.

The host started, "Welcome to *Your Voice* on the Talk Network. This is your host, Robert Rich, and I have with me today Jason Bigley and retired Colonel Samuel Sloan. Jason, as most of you know, wrote the article published on the website *The Whole Truth!* which has everyone talking. In that article, Jason takes to task the United States government for its failure to inform citizens of the dangers presented by Chinese militarization of orbital space.

Looking directly into the camera he said, “According to Jason, ladies and gentlemen, we are all at the mercy of our Chinese overlords.”

The camera caught Colonel Sloan wincing at the hyperbole.

“Also with me is former Space Command Colonel Samuel Sloan. Colonel Sloan is here to argue against Jason's conclusions. I would like to start the discussion by asking Jason for a quick rundown of his remarkable reporting.”

Jason began well, providing a quick review of the main points of his web story. He closed his comments by assuring the viewers that each major point of his story could be confirmed by an independent source if necessary.

Rich turned to Colonel Sloan and said, “So Colonel from what I just heard, Jason's reporting seems to be sound. What exactly is your objection to his story.”

“My understanding of journalism is that you print the facts. And the facts are two. First, the hypersonic fleet of the United States has been placed on alert, but this is not unusual. Second, that the Chinese are intending to conduct a system-wide review of their military forces, sometimes called war games, this is also not unusual.

“Now Mr. Bigley has decided these two events are connected. But I can assure the viewers that besides the coincidence of these two events they have no other relation. I repeat, they are only coincidences, there is no rational connection between the two. Everyone I know in the military or formerly in the military will say the same thing.”

Rich said, “Thank you Colonel, that was a bit much, but I think we all understand your position now. Jason, do you have a response to what the Colonel has just said.”

“Yes, I would point out that the Colonel did not deny the

main points of my story. In fact, he confirmed them. I would also like to point out that though he calls the timing of these two events a coincidence, he does not deny that the timing is unusual. To put the hypersonic forces of the United States on high alert is not an inconsequential event. To call for massive war games as the Chinese have done is also not of inconsequential significance. Are we to believe that these two countries, now allies but formerly enemies, have by coincidence essentially put their military forces on high alert? Are we to believe there is no connection? Isn't it more reasonable to assume that the two events are connected? Isn't it safer for the security of this country to assume there is a connection? Isn't it patriotic to assume such? Is the Colonel such a patriot?"

"Now wait a minute young man. Your insinuation is too much for me to take without objection. Tell me, what branch of the services did you serve in?"

Rich smiled.

"Colonel Sloan knows that I did not have the honor to serve my country. However, I do not see how that impacts the truth. My story ..."

"Your story," said the Colonel interrupting. "Your story is not based on truth but conjecture. The connection between the two events in question has no basis in fact but only in fiction. Your fiction Mr. Bigley."

"Colonel let me ask you a question. Were you not at one time a source of military information for me?"

"When you acted in a responsible manner, yes I shared information with you."

"Then do you deny that you were contacted by someone in the US military ordering you to not share any more information with me when I started trying to find out the reason behind the US hypersonic forces being brought to high alert?"

"Yes, and I did so because I am, unlike you, a patriot."

"Oh," said Jason. "So, it's patriotic to withhold information from citizens and unpatriotic to tell those citizens the truth? Is that the position you are taking?"

"Before you answer Colonel," said Rich. "We need to take a break."

Turning to the camera Rich said, "We'll be right back."

Rich turned to his guests and said, "I thought that was an excellent segment gentleman. Keep it up in the next segment and we should get great ratings."

Just then Rich's assistant ran up and handed him a note.

"Damn!" said Rich after reading the note. "Damn it, I can't believe it. The show didn't go out. The satellite is down. Something is happening up there."

CHAPTER 14

Back in Donner's room he and his dad found that many of the satellites Donner had located were off-line. A few internet radios were still operating and from these, they heard the news. Someone had attacked the space assets of the United States. Commercial assets belonging to US multinationals were also under attack. No one had found an obvious sign of rockets or missile explosions (other than the explosion of the satellites themselves) so most speculated the attacker used kinetic energy weapons. Such weapons, launched by electromagnetic railguns, would offer greater stealth at launch and be more difficult to track than conventional rockets, especially if launched in large numbers.

If this were true, then it was also expected that these weapons had been launched from the moon or its vicinity. No one knew who had launched the attack but there were just a few suspects since there were few bases on the moon. The US, China, Japan and India all had moon bases. Most commentators suspected Chinese involvement.

A few denounced the attack as deplorable, but many others argued that it was only just, as the US had for many years been the world's greatest aggressor. Donner and his dad gave up on getting any factual information and shut down the setup.

"We'll check later Donner, as far as this bunch knows it could have been caused by little green men," said Jack shaking his head.

The talk at dinner was about what might have happened. Donner's mother seemed particularly disturbed at the news of war. Jack carefully explained that they hadn't enough information to verify that what had happened was an act of war. And he suspected that even if it was an act of aggression, it wouldn't directly affect them except maybe as an increase in food prices. It would, therefore, make even more sense to try and farm enough to support the three of them.

After dinner, Donner and his dad went back up into his room

to listen for any news. Some of the geostationary satellites they had found earlier seemed to be off-line now. After several minutes of searching low Earth orbit satellites, they found what seemed to be an official broadcast from the White House. The president's spokesman read the following statement:

"At five-fifty PM Eastern Standard Time, the space resources of the United States were put under attack. This includes military and commercial assets. This attack was unprovoked. Five minutes later thousands of hypersonic aircraft and missiles were launched against our ground and sea assets. Our allies in the Polish block and India were also attacked. The attack heavily damaged the United States' capability to respond. However, using other assets untouched by the first attack, US systems detected the launch locations of this second wave of attacks. They came from Japanese and Turkish controlled territories. At six-ten PM the President ordered a retaliatory strike against these launch sites and other strategic sites with our remaining hypersonic resources. Just a few minutes ago at eight-twenty PM the Japanese and Turks confirmed our intelligence by broadcasting terms of surrender to Washington. The President has rejected these terms but agreed to negotiate. It is unknown at this time as to the extent of the damages to our forces or the loss of life, we will release these numbers when we have them. The President will be making a speech at nine-thirty PM, I urge all Americans to tune in. That is all for now."

The press yelled questions at the spokesman, but he was gone, and the broadcast went back to the local anchors.

"Is it all over now?" asked Donner.

"I suspect this first wave of the war is over. The hypersonic weapons they used travel at Mach 5 or greater, that's about four-thousand miles-per-hour. And with precision guidance it doesn't take long for targets anywhere in the world to be taken out."

"Why dad, why did they do it?"

"Well son, I can tell you that the Japanese have been hard-pressed to maintain their standard of living since the turn of the century, mostly because of their decreasing population, especially the working-age population. They obviously want to gain access to resources, and they apparently believe the US is preventing them from doing so. I don't know why the Turks are involved but they are a relatively young country and could have similar resource pressures. Or maybe the Turks are trying to become a regional power, and they feel the US is blocking their efforts. It will be some time before we know for sure."

"What about the military space assets we lost, what are those dad? I thought we hadn't any except for some military satellites?"

"That too is something we will be learning about over the next several days or weeks Donner. It might be military satellites, but I suspect it has something to do with the radio source you found. And I am sure that radio source is what prompted the Japanese and Turks into taking action and choosing this time to do it. Let's wait until we hear what the President has to say."

The President's address just reiterated what the spokesman had said earlier. The only new piece of information was that negotiations would begin in Geneva in a week. He urged all Americans to remain calm.

"I'm going down to your mother," said Jack. "Don't stay up late, we will probably learn more tomorrow anyway, goodnight."

"Goodnight dad," said Donner. Donner set his system up to scan and laid on his bed where he went to sleep listening to snippets of the news.

CHAPTER 15

Donner continued his scans for news the following morning. He noted that the remaining operational satellites that he could scan were either foreign-owned or were part of an international communications network. Apparently, the Japanese had been very careful with their target selection, choosing only those that were directly owned by the US government and US corporations, and only when they weren't involved in broadcasting to a broader global audience.

But collateral damage had been extensive. US television services were particularly hard hit. Most American TV networks had to rely on internet streaming to continue operations. In any event, they estimated that half their former audience was unable to receive their broadcasts. The broadcast corporations demanded compensation for their losses but were ignored as they didn't have the influence to stir up public opinion anymore.

The negotiations began a week later in Geneva. On one side was the US, India, Poland and their allies; on the other side were Japan and Turkey and their allies. Days passed without any agreements, only accusations. The Japanese presented evidence of the militarization of space by the United States. They contended that the US had secretly tried to construct three command and control platforms in geosynchronous orbit, one above South America, one off the coast of Africa with Turkey in view and one above the Pacific south of Japan.

The Japanese claimed these platforms had offensive and electronic jamming capabilities that essentially reduced the warning time for hypersonic missiles aimed at Japan to a few minutes instead of the former half hour. The Japanese and Turks pointed out that the establishment of these military platforms and their offensive capabilities were against international law and was provocative enough to warrant their actions.

The Japanese presented evidence that the Washington-Beijing-Seoul alliance that had emerged in the past decade had led to the necessary growth of the Japanese military. They claimed they were being denied a clear and safe supply line for the imported resources that they desperately needed to maintain their economy.

Turkey complained that the instability in its local area was not being addressed by any of the major powers and it was up to them to stabilize the region for their own safety as well as the safety of neighboring states. The US military's projection of power was in direct defiance of this basic need while not contributing anything to its fulfillment. The orbiting "Battle Stars," as the Turks labeled them, was the provocation that forced them to act.

Donner now understood the importance of those messages he had intercepted. They were updates on the Battle Stars to Japanese Intelligence.

The US and its allies denied all the charges. They termed the Japanese and Turkish actions as bald aggression and paranoid delusions.

The talks were obviously not going well. Donner was astounded at the lack of sincerity on both sides. He soon stopped listening to the news preferring to spend his days helping his dad prepare the farm as much as possible for self-sufficiency.

Donner and his dad were working in the barn, building more stalls to hold the animals that Jack hoped to buy. The robotic carpenter was excellent at cutting boards just right even though it didn't physically measure the cuts. Donner and his dad then nailed the boards up.

Donner said, "Dad, before I stopped following them the talks in Geneva just seemed to be a lot of accusations, no one really wanted to address the issues honestly it seemed to me."

"Yes Donner. There is always a lot of posturing in any kind of negotiations. What they are doing is trying to influence public opinion so that any agreement will seem necessary and reasonable and the parties to the negotiations will appear blameless, no matter the nature of the treaty that comes out of the negotiations."

"So, they don't actually want to solve problems just make sure people don't blame them for the results?"

"Something like that."

"You know dad I've been thinking that instead of going to school for a doctorate, maybe I'll just get a bachelor's and try to make a career in flying. You know how much I love flying."

"If that is what you want son. I think you should always pursue your interests and not society's. Too many people doing things they don't like already."

"That's what I think too dad."

CHAPTER 16

Lieutenant Armstrong had been one of the lucky ones. When his Battle Star was first hit by the kinetic energy weapon, essentially a long spike of nano-hardened carbon fiber, he had responded to the abandon ship alarm by taking the nearest ladder to the wheel's perimeter. He had come off the ladder right next to a lifeboat pod. He waited until the station was shaking violently and when he saw no one else, he accessed the pod and launched it.

Brently was quite far away from the platform when he saw the next hit. The inertia wheel where his private quarters were seemed to wobble noticeably as if it were a top spinning down. Next, he saw the spine of the platform buckle.

The bottom boom, the part pointed toward Earth, began folding almost in its middle. Brently watched the tip of the boom and its attachments approaching the wobbling wheel in slow motion. Brently wanted to yell, to warn, as he watched the end of the boom shred into the wheel. That was when the wheel started disintegrating, throwing off chunks of itself. Rooms and equipment he could easily recognize from this distance, but thankfully not the bodies, human or robot.

Brently stopped watching the destruction of the platform; he knew that the pod was recording it anyway. He turned to look at his destination. A stable low orbit around the moon from which he hoped to be rescued in a few days.

CHAPTER 17

September 6, 2054

Three weeks after negotiations had begun, the US used its remaining space-based assets and secret ground-based weapons to launch an attack on the Japanese-Turkish coalition in space. Within two hours, the coalition's space assets were essentially destroyed. The coalition was now blind. Then the US launched its remaining hypersonic airplanes and delivered almost total destruction to the remaining military assets of Japan and Turkey. The peace talks were suspended.

It was zero six hundred, early dawn, when the alarm went off on base. Emily bolted upright in her bunk. That was the launch alarm. She wondered what was going on.

No one had told her anything about a launch. Of course, she was still on report and didn't have any reason to expect to be informed. Still, Emily felt she should have been told. She had to get down to the hangar and check on the hypersonics. She quickly dressed.

The air was still comfortably cool around the hangar. The security guard saluted, apparently not aware of Emily's status. Inside the control room, where Emily should have been, she could see all the top brass. Emily entered the door code and went into the wiring closet down the hall. She took out the alligator clips with the makeshift connector at one end that she had used for troubleshooting many times. She found the terminals marked COMM-BASE23-HYPER1. That was Looker's military designation. She hooked the alligator clips to the terminals and plugged the other end into her Annie.

Emily whispered into her Annie, "Looker this is Sg, over."

Emily waited.

And waited.

Surely Looker would have responded by now. She heard motion outside the door. She reached for the alligator clips but stopped when she heard, “Looker to Sg, over.”

“Looker glad to hear,” whispered Emily. “How are systems?”

“Systems nominal. How are systems, Sg?”

Emily understood then that Looker was aware of her recent absence. Emily replied, “Systems nominal, Looker, but reassigned.”

“Understood. Mission is a go; I am rolling.”

“Understood,” said Emily. She unplugged the clips and raced outside to see the takeoff.

Emily saw the first four hypersonics take off and adopt a finger-four combat formation, which was unusual. Looker must be doing that, thought Emily. Then Emily choked as the hypersonic to the right of the point pulled up in what was undoubtedly a missing man salute.

Donner and his dad heard about the new attacks when they came in from the fields that evening. Jack said, “Well, there goes any chance for a quick resolution; we're in for a long struggle.”

December 31, 2054

By the end of the year, the Turks had started a ground assault on the Polish bloc using their augmented soldier system. These were soldiers in battle suits whose robotic and computational systems gave them the equivalent fighting capacity of an entire squadron from just a few years before. Networked, they could easily sweep a large area clear of the enemy. Romania capitulated almost immediately and signed a treaty with the coalition. Hungary was overrun within a week. Slovakia put up a stubborn resistance but fell in only three days. Poland now faced the coalition directly and almost alone. The New Year looked bleak for the US and its allies.

Jacek Bukowski was caught in a no man's land. The Turkish battle suits, what the Poles called kombinezon bitwy or kombinz for short, had passed Jacek, and he was now trapped behind enemy lines. The suits in the distance looked like giants threshing the fields.

The speed with which the Turks could move in their kombinz was astounding. The Polish tanks were barely able to keep up or keep out of the way would be more descriptive. The kombinz could not only push the Poles faster than they could retreat, but could also clear such a wide area that regrouping for the Poles became impossible.

The networked battle suits, each manned by a Turkish specialist, were almost impossible to take out with small arms fire. They could be disabled with a hit by artillery, drone, or tank fire, but this was more luck than skill. Each arm held enough firepower to take out a platoon or tank with a single burst. Other Turks in battle suits ranging behind the advancing front could bring up supplies or take the place of a fallen kombinz as needed.

They never stop, thought Jacek. Always a new, refreshed kombinz to take the place in the front. "Unstoppable," he whispered from his hiding place.

Then he saw it. The weakest link in the battle suit's armor. He moved closer.

A kombinz had stopped. It was being serviced by a utility track vehicle. A Turkish soldier climbed the nearest power pole carrying what looked like thick cables. He attached the cables carefully to the power lines, the end claws digging into the sheathing. The soldiers on the ground were attaching more cables to the backpack of the kombinz.

Jacek knew what they were doing. They were recharging the battery pack of the kombinz. He would stop them.

Jacek ran down the power line away from the stalled kombinz. He found the power pole he wanted. Raising his MSBS-9,56 assault rifle, he emptied the magazine. Another clip and he had the electrical lines on the ground.

He was pleased; he had been able to do something. He wasn't running anymore.

With all the firing, Jacek hadn't noticed the kombinz coming up behind him.

Donner spent the winter in the snows that came and went and on the frozen stream that crossed the field between the house and the mountains. He didn’t think much of the war anymore. If he took to the internet, it was to research airplanes and piloting.

CHAPTER 18

January 16, 2055

The US announced that it had destroyed the launch base that the Japanese used on the moon. Japan claimed many civilian lives had been lost because of the US action. The US claimed that any Japanese civilians and military were given the option of leaving the base before the attack, and that only a few of the more zealous Japanese military had remained.

Lt. Danner looked at the video display of the hopper rocket; there below were the Japanese railguns, exactly where he had expected to find them. The EM detection equipment he maintained had triangulated the location precisely. At first, he had been confused as to the cause of the large EM pulses he had observed, but after hearing about the attack on the Battle Stars, he had suspected the pulses and the destruction of the Battle Stars were related.

He knew the order came from headquarters, but at first Lt. Danner thought the captain was crazy, expecting him to find the railguns and the Japanese base and neutralize them. After all, they weren't really up here to fight a war; most of the men on the base were specialists. He had had only a short time to prepare but came up with a plan before liftoff.

The hopper rocket reached the spot triangulated and set down close to the railgun machinery. Lt. Danner explained to his men what he wanted them to do while he and Sergeant Norris inspected the railgun controls.

The guns were operated remotely from the Japanese base but had local controls also. Sergeant Norris used his somewhat rusty Japanese language skills to decipher the control panel. By the time the men had completed the Lieutenant's orders, Norris believed he could also operate the guns remotely using his Annie.

Everything was ready; Lt. Danner asked Norris to establish radio contact with the Japanese base and give them the ultimatum. They had one hour to surrender or suffer the consequences. The reply from the base was somewhat rude and vulgar, if the Sergeant had interpreted it correctly. The Lieutenant was unperturbed; he would give them a chance and wait.

The hopper rocket had moved over the horizon about two and a half kilometers from the gun installation. The hour was up. The Lieutenant gave the Sergeant the order, and his Annie sent the order to the railguns to charge. All six railguns tried to charge simultaneously. The Japanese power station hadn't been built to handle the load. Though automatic cutoffs should have kicked in, the Lieutenant's men had bypassed them.

It was the first storm ever seen on the moon as the railguns disintegrated blindingly against the dark of space.

They would fly the hopper rocket back over the gun installation and the Japanese base to take pictures and pick up any survivors that had decided to surrender. But the Lieutenant knew from the visible display that millions of amps of current had accomplished the mission.

Donner began asking his dad about his student flight license. Would they still be able to get it with the war ongoing? His dad assured him that as far as he knew the license was still being issued and Donner would get his on his sixteenth birthday in August.

March 13, 2055

In March, the US launched airstrikes on the Turkish army

advancing into Poland. Casualties were high. In April the Germans moved against the Poles with the encouragement of the Turks. The Russians left weakened after years of a bad economy, refused to be drawn into the struggle. By May, the British, with an almost intact air force, entered the war against the coalition, flying sorties against the advancing German armies in Poland.

Amir Atakan held the rank of Ustegaman in the Turkish military, equivalent to a First Lieutenant in the US Air Force. He had been in his battle suit now for two days without relief. The attacks from the air and the supply difficulties had finally caught up with the Turkish forces.

Amir had watched in disbelief as the Poles had deliberately destroyed their power system. He could understand such actions from a military strategy point of view. But such deliberate destruction not only affected military combatants but also the civilian population. The Poles were willing to endanger the lives of their families, their wives and children. Would he have the nerve to do such a thing if Turkey were threatened? He didn't know. One part of him admired the Poles' dedication; the civilized part of him was repulsed.

But he had more immediate worries. His battery pack was getting dangerously low. Without that power, he would be stuck in this field without defenses. He had called for a backup supply, but they were certainly taking their time.

Then he saw movement at the edge of the field. He saw the Polish soldiers emerge from the woods. But he relaxed when he saw they weren't carrying anything other than their assault rifles. The battle suit could easily handle those weapons, thought Amir.

He went to work.

As usual, the Poles were dropping with ease. The suit could take on more than two dozen targets at a time and coordinate the return fire. With Amir focusing on the battle, he didn't notice the soft alarm as the battle suit began to shut down. The bullets slamming the suit's bulletproof sheathing began to sound like a hard rain as the suit went silent.

Then the Poles stopped firing as they noticed the battle suit had stopped. Amir was feverishly working to extricate himself from the suit when he saw one of the Poles stand up and walk toward him. In the suit, he stood nearly six feet above the head of the approaching Pole. Amir could see the young man's face. He saw him detach a grenade from the grenade belt which he wore across his shoulder like a sling. Amir was transfixed as the young man pulled the pin from the grenade and gently laid it at the suit's feet. He then slowly backpedaled, all the while staring fiercely into Amir's eyes. Then Amir saw another Polish soldier approaching, reaching for a grenade; then Amir saw the first young man and the approaching soldier hit the ground, then Amir felt the concussive force of the explosion at his feet and saw the field disappear in smoke and flying debris, and that was the last he saw.

Donner began lobbying his dad to build a runway in the field. He pointed out that their plane would only need at most five hundred meters to take off at the altitude of the farm. And a hard-packed grass field would be excellent, and it wouldn't take much to build a hangar for storage. His dad listened but pointed out the difficulty of creating a smooth enough surface for the plane. Donner argued that it would only take maybe a week with some heavy earth moving equipment and a professional who knew how to use it. His dad was noncommittal, but Donner noticed he didn't say no right away.

August 22, 2055

By August, the Poles had deliberately destroyed their power generation capability, plunging the entire nation into darkness. The Turks and Germans had depended on this power-generating capability to keep their battery-powered, highly robotic forces moving. Without the ability to easily charge the power packs, the military advance stumbled as they frantically sought other ways to supply the troopers over lengthening supply lines.

That August, the runway was finished, as was the hangar, and Donner and his dad had flown their airplane into the valley. Donner applied for his student license and began to fly under his dad's tutelage.

CHAPTER 19

Donner started his last year of study at the local high school to get as many math and science courses as he could. By doing so, he would graduate a year early. He'd already applied to study aeronautical engineering. Except for price inflation on food and some other goods, the war was far away and out of his thoughts.

His fellow students avidly discussed each new bit of news from the battlefield. But when they asked Donner what he thought, he usually said, "You know I don't follow it too much; it will eventually be over, and to be honest, I don't think anything will be settled. I'm more interested in graduating and getting my pilot license. Maybe by then, the war will be over, and we won't have to speculate. The only thing I'm sure of is that this war will lead to another."

Donner's response usually led the questioner to doubt Donner's patriotism, but it wasn't as much a lack of patriotism as it was a mature and well-developed realism. Donner knew history as well as his beloved aeronautics. And he knew the nation-state had not existed in the past and no doubt would cease to exist in the future.

What would continue to exist were the men and women that made up that state. Though young he had already learned that a person's life is well spent providing for others not in the mass but in the particular.

The war ended as Donner was starting his last semester of high school. The US, after rebuilding its air and space assets, launched a massive assault on the Turkish-Japanese coalition, stopping just short of complete annihilation of the opposing forces. It then offered terms of surrender that the Turks and Japanese had no choice but to accept.

Just as Donner had said the war settled nothing, the US was still the reigning superpower after the war as before, and the Turks and Japanese still faced the same resource and security problems that they had gone to war to solve. Much destruction and the lives of almost fifty thousand people were the only clear outcomes of the war.

Donner got his pilot license and graduated high school with honors. He was well prepared to study engineering and pursue his love of flying.

After his graduation party, Donner and his dad talked.

“Dad, do you think the world will ever learn that war isn't the answer to its problems?”

“No, Donner I don't, as long as people are as imperfect as they are. And they are not going to change in this world, maybe the next, but not in this one; that's for sure.”

“Those that don't want to fight have nowhere to go to avoid conflict.”

“That's true. Except maybe the Mars colonists. They may be far enough from this system of things to avoid the machinations of the world. The moon, though, is too close.”

“I'd like to go to Mars someday,” said Donner.

“I would too,” said his dad.

LOOKING BACK

War Through The Pines was written at the end of 2015 and published the next year. It had its genesis in the book ***The Next Hundred Years*** by George Friedman, published in 2009. In that book, he predicts the next world war to occur around the middle of the twenty-first century.

As with most wars, it is fought over resources. The general outline of that conflict was followed, and specifics such as the Battle Stars and the Battle Suits the Turkish used, but I don't remember if they were named that in the book.

Hypersonic airplanes and drones were known but not implemented to any degree when the story was written. We are still waiting for hypersonics to become common, but drones are very familiar from the war between Russia and the Ukraine. They have completely changed the battlefield, even if the huge Battle Suits haven't appeared yet. One of the interesting things is that in his book, Friedman predicts that the casualties and deaths in the war will be tens of thousands, instead of the millions of the last world war. This is a result of robotics and AI, and I follow his lead in the story. Deaths are relatively low, but destruction is relatively high in this future war.

Donner's mother and dad should be familiar from the first novelette in the series, ***Whatsoever You Do***, where they were main characters. I've been accused of not providing character arcs in my stories, just a day to day telling of events, but if Donner's change in outlook isn't a character arc, then I'm baffled.

Finally, the technology that Donner uses and becomes proficient in is from my fifty-year background in electronics. Though it may seem remarkable for so young a boy to master, I've seen some near examples in my time in the field.

Interestingly, I projected ubiquitous satellite access in the story. Starlink from SpaceX had been announced at the time of the writing, but it was four years later before any of the satellites were launched. Now, they are talking about tens of thousands, if not hundreds of thousands, of such low-earth-orbit satellites. Also, in all these stories I projected artificial intelligence assistants, and now we have almost exactly these entities.

These days it's difficult to write near-future science fiction while keeping ahead of the technology curve.

THANK YOU FOR READING

Continue your journey to the stars with the next book of the 11 volume ***From The Earth Series****:*

Vigilance

The history of freedom repeats itself. And the costs are always the same.

The settlers of the new Republic of Mars were in a struggle for their freedom against powerful forces that would stop at nothing.

For the Martians the costs were life, property and domestic security. But the true cost was vigilance, eternal if need be.

Vigilance is set in the future (2070s) and is the third story in the **From The Earth Series** which itself is set in the much larger **Future Chron Universe.**

See the author's website ***www.dwpatterson.com*** for availability and more.

Hard Science Fiction – Old School.

THE FUTURE CHRON UNIVERSE

My first "universe," **Future Chron**, is complete at this time. It consists of 8 short stories, 15 novelettes, 1 novella, and 9 novels. It is generally a far future universe.

I had been writing in this universe since the end of 2015 until the last novel was published in 2022.

While plot and character drive the storytelling in the **Future Chron** universe (I think), physics also plays an important role. However, this is not known physics but highly extrapolated future physics. (Actually, the universe starts in the near future when technology and science is not much different from now).

But this extrapolated physics is not "just made up" but has its genesis in current research or popular science books. This is an important point to me, although it may seem to be "made up" science and technology, it has the possibility, however slightly, to come true. At least, at this point to my knowledge, nothing I've written can be ruled out.

Here is the recommended reading order for the first eleven stories.

FROM THE EARTH SERIES:

The **From The Earth Series** consists of 10 novelettes and one novella. These are the foundational stories of the Future Chron Universe. They follow mankind's journey from Earth to the stars (Alpha Centauri anyway).

Whatsoever You Do - 2032 - Novelette

A pandemic had long been predicted.

Now it was happening and a former graduate student, Jack Jackson, may have the key to its containment, synthetic biology.

But because in the court of public opinion synthetic biology is feared, it has been forbidden in the money conscious halls of medical research.

How many will have to die before they change their minds?

War Through The Pines - 2044 – Novelette

What starts in space may not stay in space.

Many governments today are preparing for war in space. Most people today are unaware of it.

When will it happen? How will it be conducted? What will be the effect on a young boy just coming of age?

Vigilance - 2071 - Novelette

The history of freedom repeats itself.

And the costs are always the same.

The settlers of the new Republic of Mars were in a struggle for their freedom against powerful forces that would stop at nothing. For the Martians the costs were life, property and domestic security.

But the true cost was vigilance, eternal if need be.

To Tend And Watch Over - 2081 - Novelette

Sometimes you don't know you aren't free until the state's coercive force is used against you.

And then you learn you are only free to do what big brother wants.

Davide Jackson was not as adventurous as the others in his clan. He was more a stay-at-home type. But that doesn't mean he longs any less to be free.

He just has to learn the cost of freedom.

Union - 2090 – Novelette

How far out into the Solar System would you have to run from authoritarian powers to be free?

The answer is that there is no place safe from the powers that would try to control you.

But in numbers, in cooperation, in pledging mutual support and fidelity, freedom might be had. For a price.

And that price is resistance, body and spirit, to those that would endeavor to control.

Circle Of Retribution - 2140 - Novelette

Gardener Jackson was one of the best pilots to ever come out of Mars Space Academy.

He was a natural to fly the missions that would mine Saturn's upper atmosphere for the fusion fuel, Helium 3, that the Solar System needed.

But there was one problem, a foe he didn't even suspect would stop at nothing to prevent Gardener from succeeding, including life-threatening sabotage.

Freedom From Want - 2153 – Novelette

The promise of Artificial Intelligence is great.

But only if Artificial Intelligence fulfills our expectations.

But what about AI's expectations? Will they be different from ours? Will AI come to believe the best way to fulfill our expectations is to manage our expectations?

If so, what of freedom?

Break Up - 2165 – Novelette

The future is predictable if not knowable and the past will repeat itself, if not in all particulars.

We know that countries have crumbled in the past and it is certain to happen again in the future.

We may think this time will be different, no doubt people in the past thought the same until their world fell apart.

Kuiper Station - 2230 – Novelette

What appeared to be a simple but ambitious goal of establishing a new colony in the Kuiper Belt, a colony to service mining activities there, was more than it seemed.

One side, led by the Solar Federation and the Jackson family, was determined to break humanity out of its centuries long stagnation and push it to embrace the stars.

The other side, led by the Terran Federation, was determined to block such expansion and maintain its power.

It would be close but the stars were calling.

The Cloud - 2328 – Novelette

It was the most audacious undertaking ever conceived by man. The building of a system-spanning Starway where giant light-sails would journey on beams of laser-light to distant stars. Not only a pathway to the stars but also an abode of life, the Starway included many space habitats built to maintain its great light focusing arrays.

But there was misunderstanding along the Starway. Misunderstanding between the Starway Corporation and the settlements.

And misunderstanding always leads to disaster.

First Interstellar - 2340 - Novella

It was a mission that no one but a Jackson would consider. But Ajax was reluctant, he had never lead such a mission, taking a lightsail powered starship from Earth to the Centauri System using the incomplete Star Way. He thought that strong leadership would be needed. He was right.

The leader would have to handle the normal amount of human drama, both petty and serious. He would also have to handle the accidents and incidents that would occur on a years long mission. But on this mission he would have to handle something else; direct sabotage by unknown individuals and indirect sabotage as a result of the crew's boredom and dereliction of duty.

Ajax would have to grow as a leader and a person if the Starway Centauri mission was to succeed.

www.ingramcontent.com/pod-product-compliance
Lightning Source LLC
LaVergne TN
LVHW050602160826
845677LV00011B/2433

9798223502487